*"MOST OF HER
FIGHTER PILOTS DYING
FROM AN UNKNOWN
VIRUS, AN ALL BUT
DEFENSELESS BATTLESTAR
GALACTICA LEADS THE
FINAL REMNANTS OF
MANKIND INTO A DARK
AND TRACKLESS VOID..."*

BATTLESTAR GALACTICA™★
Marvel Comics Group Presents:

BATTLESTAR GALACTICA™★ Copyright©1979 Universal City Studios, Inc. Comics and text copyright©1979 by Universal City Studios, Inc. All Rights Reserved.
★ BATTLESTAR GALACTICA™★ is a trademark of and licensed by Universal City Studios, Inc.
Developed by the Marvel Comics Group, a division of Cadence Industries Corp. under license from Universal City Studios, Inc.
ISBN: 0-441-04877-3
Tempo Books is registered in the U.S. Patent Office
Published simultaneously in Canada
Printed in the United States of America

Based on the television series
BATTLESTAR GALACTICA™★ created by Glen Larson.

STAN LEE PRESENTS:

BattlestaR GALACTICA

VOLUME II

A Tempo Star Book
Distributed by Ace Books
Grosset & Dunlap, Inc., Publishers
New York, N.Y. 10010
A Filmways Company

Edited by	Allen L. Milgrom
Written by	Roger McKenzie
Penciled by	Walt Simonson and Rich Buckler
Inked by	Klaus Janson
Colored by	Carl Gafford, Glynis Wein, Klaus Janson
Lettered by	Jim Novak

* * * * * * * * * * * * * * * *

Editor-in-Chief, Marvel Comics Group	Jim Shooter
Assistant Editor	Mary Jo Duffy
Art Director	Marie Severin
Production Manager	Len Grow
Assistant Production Manager	Danny Crespi
Coloring Supervision	Andy Yanchus

* * * * * * * * * * * * * * * *

Production supervised by	Sol Brodsky
Layout & mechanicals by	Carl Wirshba, Alex Soma
Production Staff:	Nel Yomtov, Irene Vartanoff, Mike Higgins, Ron Zalme, Elaine Heinl, Jose Albelo, Mark Rogan, Stan Aaron, Elliot Brown
COVER ART	Rich Buckler and Klaus Janson
Cover colored by	George Roussos

I'M EITHER GOING TO FIND YOU, CAPTAIN, OR...

AND SEVERAL CENTONS LATER...

WHAT THE--?! LASER BURSTS! IS THAT YOU, STARBUCK?

STARBUCK?

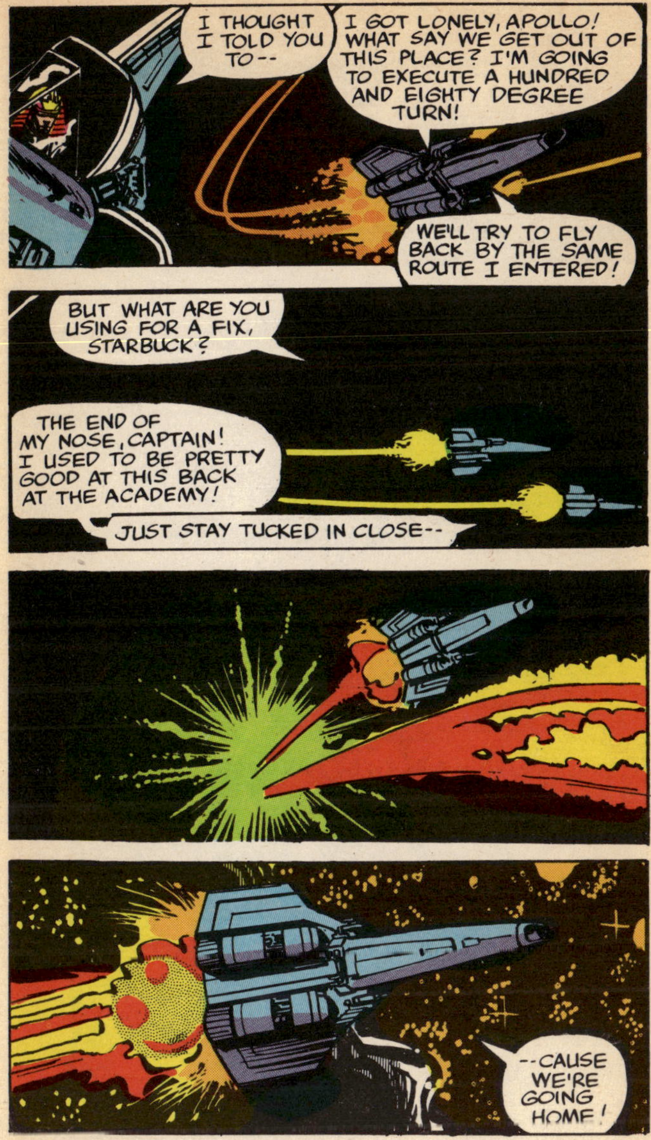

AT THAT MOMENT, ABOARD A CYLON BASE STAR--

--IN THE COMMAND CHAMBER OF THE IMPERIOUS LEADER...

I HAVE EXAMINED YOUR EPISTLE SUGGESTING YOU WOULD BE ABLE TO LOCATE THE HUMANS, BALTAR!

O-OH, YES, IMPERIOUS LEADER! I...I THINK AS THEY DO! I KNOW WHERE THEY MUST GO, WHAT THEY MUST DO!

YOUR REASONING IS MOST...LOGICAL!

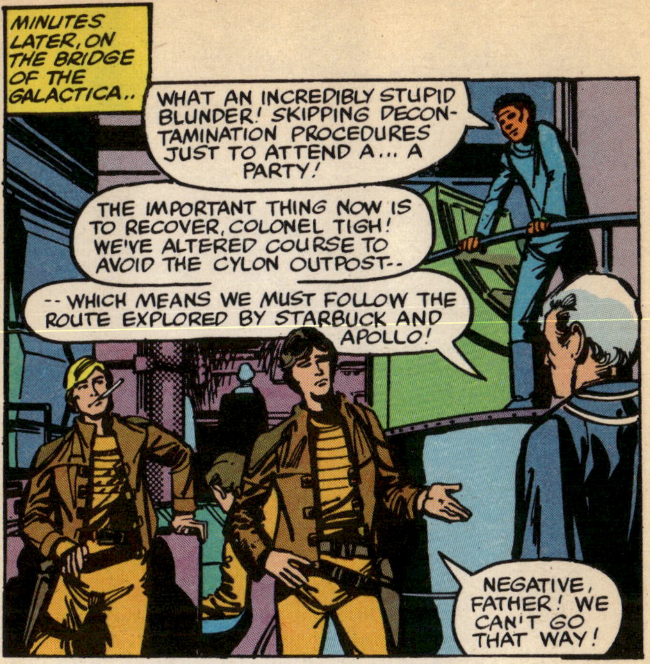

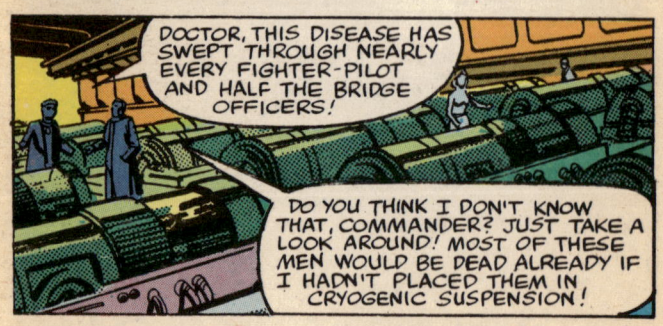

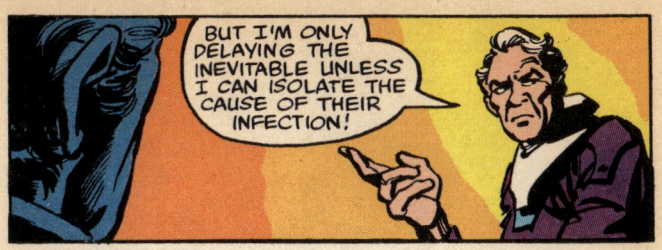

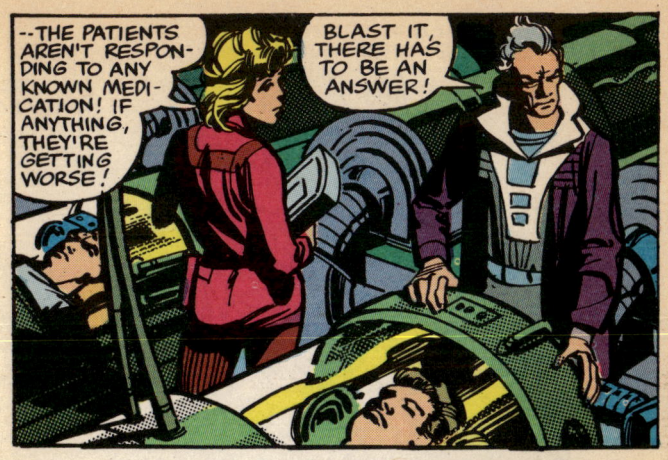

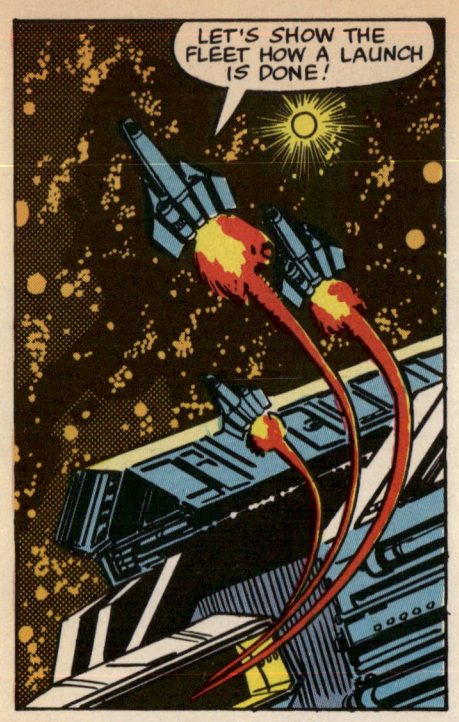

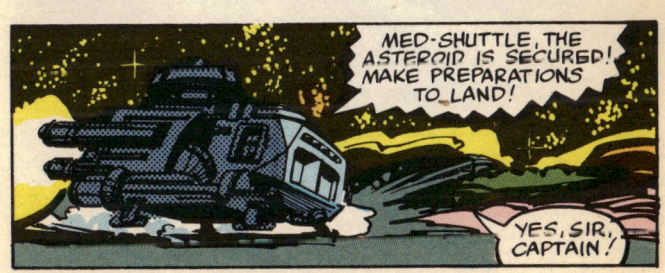

THE LOST GODS OF KOBOL -- PART TWO
A DEATH IN THE FAMILY!

MOST OF HER FIGHTER PILOTS *DYING* FROM AN UNKNOWN VIRUS, AN ALL-BUT DEFENSELESS BATTLESTAR GALACTICA LEADS THE FINAL REMNANTS OF MANKIND INTO A DARK AND TRACKLESS VOID--

--DESPERATELY ATTEMPTING TO ESCAPE THE RELENTLESS PURSUIT OF THE *CYLONS*, A MERCILESS, ALIEN ENEMY THAT HAS STALKED THEM ACROSS HALF A GALAXY!

COMMANDER ADAMA, THE MEDICAL SHUTTLE IS RETURNING FROM ASTEROID BETA-SEVEN--

A ROGER McKENZIE • WALTER SIMONSON • KLAUS JANSON MARVEL MASTERWORK!

NOVAK, LETTERING
ALLEN MILGROM, EDITOR
JIM SHOOTER, EDITOR-IN-CHIEF

"--AND JUST IN TIME, TOO! THIS MAGNETIC SEA IS A NAVIGATIONAL NIGHTMARE!"

"IF WE SHOULD BECOME LOST--"

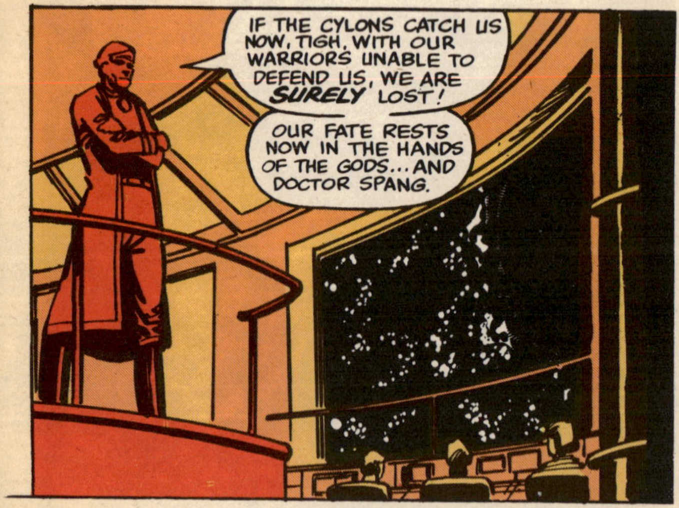

"IF THE CYLONS CATCH US NOW, TIGH, WITH OUR WARRIORS UNABLE TO DEFEND US, WE ARE *SURELY* LOST!"

"OUR FATE RESTS NOW IN THE HANDS OF THE GODS... AND DOCTOR SPANG."

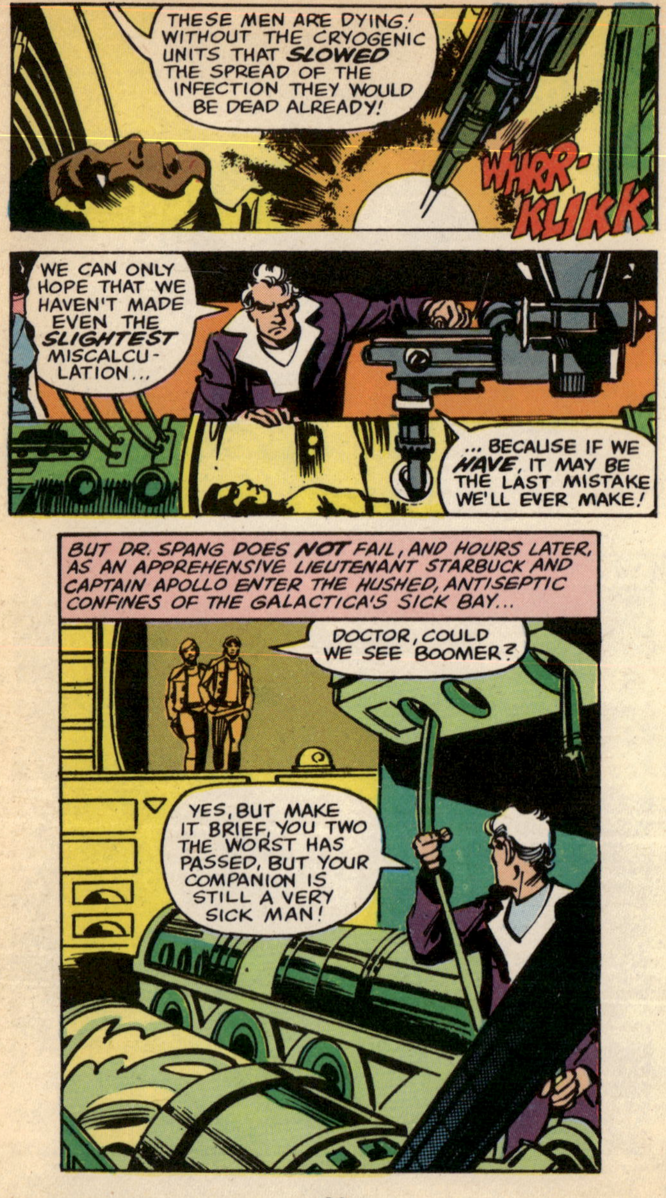

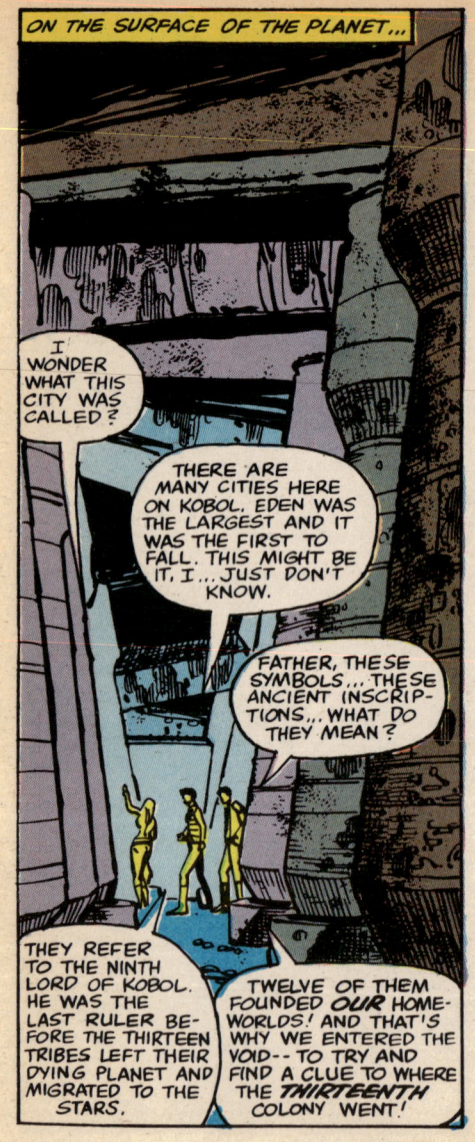

"THAT IS MY HOPE, SON. HERE, THIS INSCRIPTION SAYS: 'BEYOND THIS PORTAL LIES THE NINTH LORD OF KOBOL IN ETERNAL PEACE! ENTER UPON PAIN OF DEATH!'"

MY MEDALLION IS THE KEY.

KLEKK

AS THE ANCIENT DOOR SWINGS OPEN...

I CAN ONLY PRAY THAT HERE, WITHIN THIS ANCIENT TOMB, ON A WORLD THAT HAS BEEN DEAD FOR MILLENIA WE WILL FIND A *DIRECTION* FOR OUR DESPERATE FLIGHT TO THE STARS!

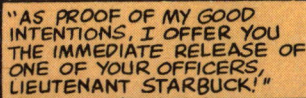

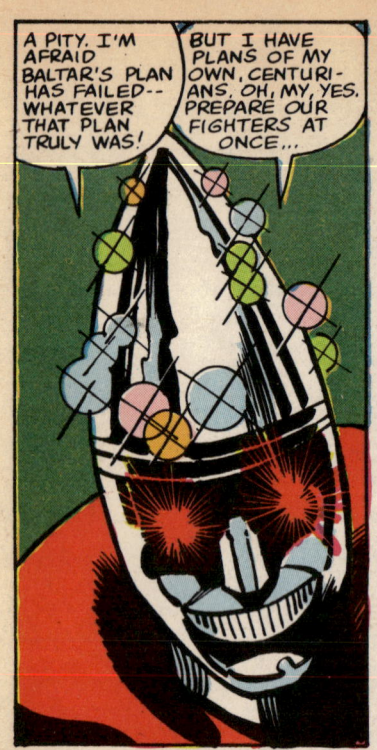

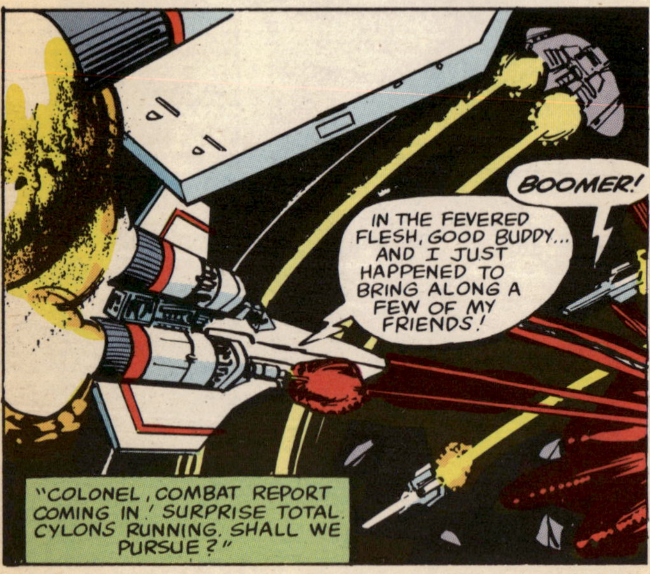

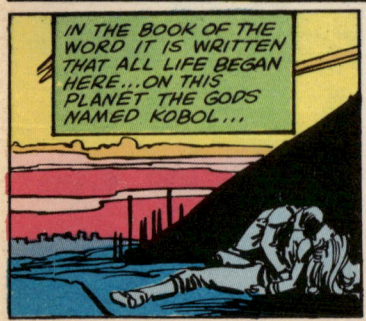

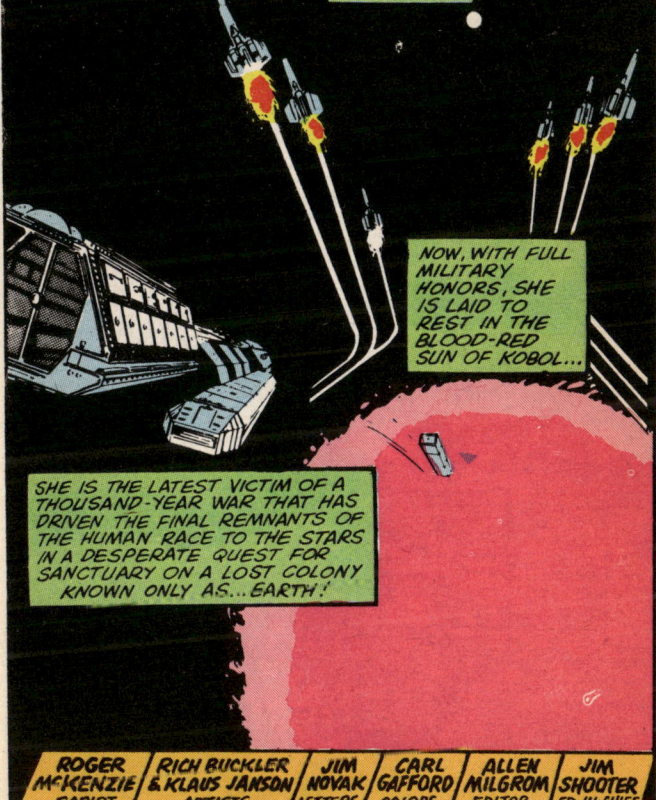

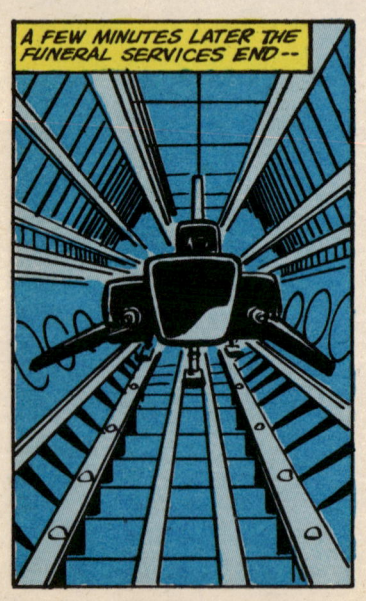

...LEADING TWO HUNDRED AND TWENTY STARSHIPS OF VARIOUS SIZES AND CONFIGURATIONS AWAY FROM ANCIENT KOBOL...

...AND EVER DEEPER INTO AN UNCHARTED VOID...

AND BARELY HAS THE RAGTAG FLEET MOVED OUT OF SCANNER RANGE, THAN, FROM THE **OPPOSITE** DIRECTION, SEVERAL CYLON FIGHTERS SHRIEK THROUGH THE ETERNAL DARKNESS!

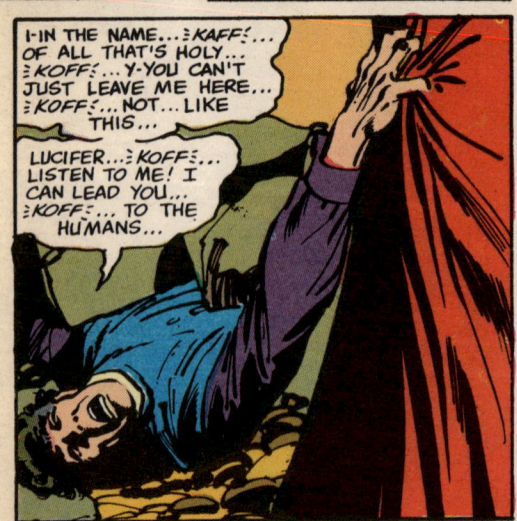

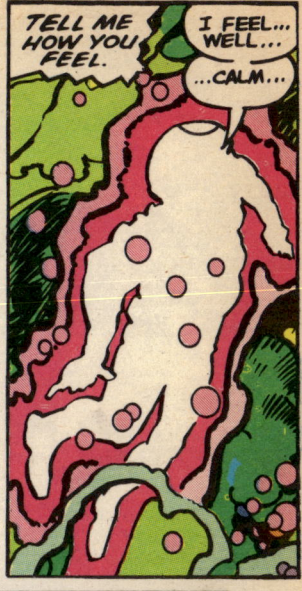

THE IMAGE IS FADING... CHANGING... I THINK...

...YES! IT'S OUR HOME ON CAPRICA! FATHER AND I RETURNED THERE... SHORTLY AFTER THE FIRST CYLON ATTACK!

HE... HE FOUND MOTHER INSIDE... BUT... IT WAS TOO LATE. THAT WAS THE ONLY TIME I EVER SAW HIM CRY...

THE PAIN OF RELIVING THESE MEMORIES MUST BE PURE TORTURE FOR MY FATHER! PLEASE, COLONEL, YOU'VE GOT TO STOP THIS--*NOW!*

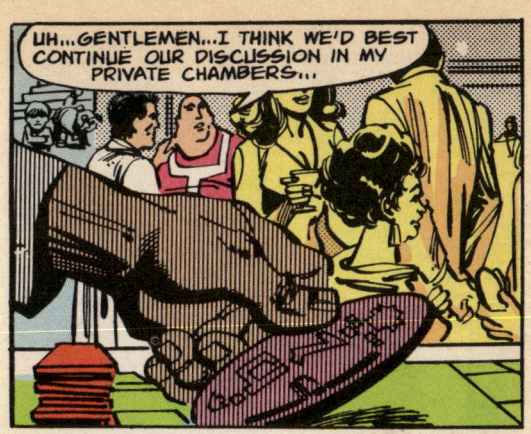